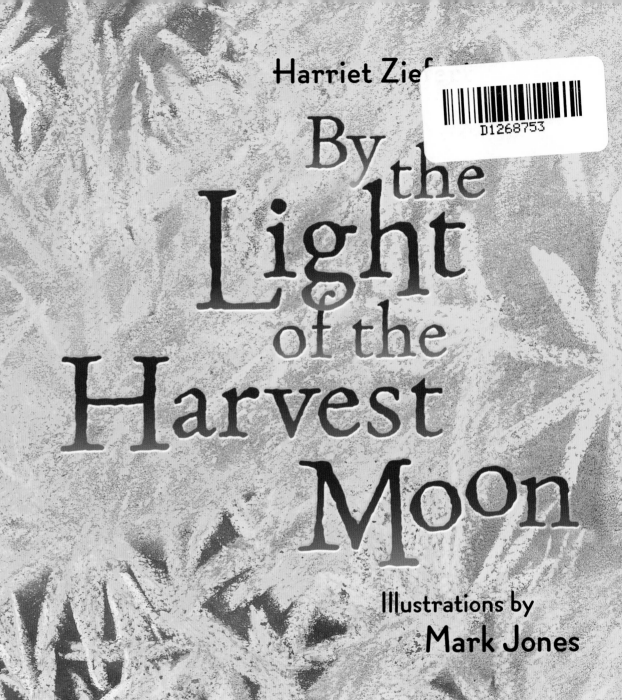

Harriet Zie[fert]

By
the
Light
of the
Harvest
Moon

Illustrations by
Mark Jones

Blue Apple Books

The harvest moon shines tonight.

Everyone is still at work
on Apple Hill Farm.

The corn is ripe since late summer
and the men and boys carry
the last of it in burlap bags
to the corn crib.

Around midnight,
one weary farmer crosses
the road and walks slowly
toward his house.
He will try to sleep. . .

though the harvest moon
still shines brightly.

The cows and the sheep stand very still.
They stare up at the orange-yellow ball,
which floats at the bottom of the sky
like a big, round balloon.

The animals talk to the moon. But she does not answer their low moos and high-pitched baas.

The wind speaks,
softly at first,
then louder.

SWISH! SWISH!

She delivers gusty blasts
of air over the fields
and farmhouse.

Orange, yellow, and
crimson leaves
swirl and twirl and dance
in the sky until . . .

a cloud of leaves settles in the pumpkin patch.
When the gusts subside,
leaf people emerge from the pile.

First come grown-ups.
Then come children. . .
and then pets.

The leaf people find a clearing and
begin decorating tables with maple leaf placemats,
golden mums, and pumpkin centerpieces.

"*Shhhh!* Hurry before
the children return,"
says a mother in a red dress.

While the grown-ups prepare,
the children play on a nearby hillside.
They bob for apples . . . juggle acorns . . .
string popcorn necklaces . . .
and weave wreaths of gold and rust-colored leaves.

The best game of all is stacking pumpkins.
One boy says, "I can stack six pumpkins."
"I can stack ten!" boasts another.
"Watch that it doesn't topple over!" warns a child.

Too late!
All the pumpkins roll
down,
down,
down the hill!

"Catch them! Stop them!"
the children shout. They chase
the runaway pumpkins
down,
down,
down the hill—
right into the middle of . . .

a party!
A dessert party!

"Surprise!"
sing the mothers and fathers,
aunts and uncles,
grandmas and grandpas.

A grandma gathers the children around.
"Today is the autumnal equinox.
The hours of daylight and darkness are equal
and fall begins. Fruits, vegetables,
and grains are harvested,
leaves turn the colors of jewels and . . ."

"We get to eat pie!"

Everyone laughs.
Then they feast
on the sweetest treats
from the fall harvest—
pumpkin, apple,
pear, and pecan pies.

Under the light of the moon
a daddy raises his glass of cider
and toasts the new season.

When the last bite of pie is eaten,
the leaf people pack everything up, join hands, and wait.

"Hold on, children.
There is still fun to be had."

The moon closes its eyes and goes to sleep.
But the wind awakens from its slumber
and delivers gusty blasts of air.

SWISH! SWISH!

The wind blows the leaf people

out of the clearing,

out of the pumpkin patch,

and into the crisp,

moonlit night.

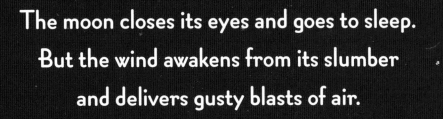
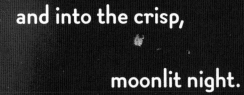

The next morning, the sun shines on Apple Hill Farm.
The farmer is in the farmhouse.
The cows and sheep are in the barn.
The leaves are in the pumpkin patch.

Everything is in its place.
If you look carefully,
you will know the leaf people
were there.